Thumbelina

First published in 2006 by
Franklin Watts
338 Euston Road
London
NW1 3BH

Franklin Watts Australia
Hachette Children's Books
Level 17/207 Kent Street
Sydney
NSW 2000

Text © Margaret Nash 2006
Illustration © Sarah Horne 2006

The rights of Margaret Nash to be identified as the author
and Sarah Horne as the illustrator of this Work have
been asserted in accordance with the Copyright, Designs
and Patents Act, 1988.

A CIP catalogue record for this book is available
from the British Library.

ISBN 0 7496 6580 7 (hbk)
ISBN 0 7496 6587 4 (pbk)

Series Editor: Jackie Hamley
Series Advisor: Dr Barrie Wade
Series Designer: Peter Scoulding

Printed in China

Thumbelina

Retold by Margaret Nash

Illustrated by Sarah Horne

FRANKLIN WATTS

LONDON • SYDNEY

Long ago, there was
a beautiful girl as tiny
as your thumb.

She was called Thumbelina.

One night, a toad stole her away and trapped her on a lily pad.

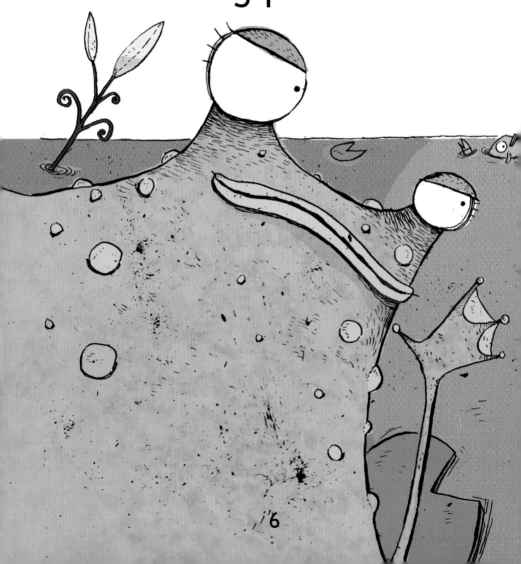

"You will marry my son!" she said. Thumbelina cried for the son was horrible.

A fish heard Thumbelina
crying and nibbled the
lily pad free.

Thumbelina floated away
and a kind butterfly pulled
her along.

Then a beetle swooped
down and grabbed
Thumbelina.

But the beetle's friends
thought she was ugly,
so he left her on a daisy.

All summer, Thumbelina listened happily to the birds singing sweetly.

But winter soon came
and Thumbelina started
to freeze.

A fieldmouse rescued her.
"You can stay with me,"
she said, "but you must
marry my friend, the mole.
He lives underground."

The mole showed
Thumbelina a dead
swallow at the end
of his tunnel.

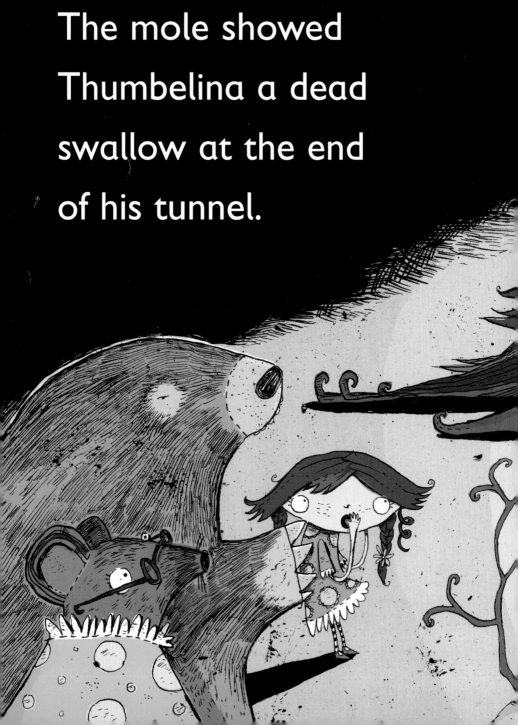

"Stupid bird!" he said,
as he kicked it.

Thumbelina kissed
the poor swallow.
"Thank you for singing
so sweetly last summer,"
she said.

19

Thumbelina made
a blanket to cover
the swallow.

As she laid it over him, the
swallow moved. He was
alive, but his wing was torn!

Thumbelina nursed the swallow better until springtime.

"Thank you, but I must go soon," he said. "What will you do?"

"I must stay here,"
said Thumbelina sadly.
"The fieldmouse is
planning my wedding
to the miserable mole."

25

The day before her wedding, Thumbelina took a long, last look at the outside world.

She would live underground
from now on. Just then,
the swallow saw her and
flew down.

"Dear Thumbelina," he said. "Do come with me!" The swallow spread his wings, and Thumbelina climbed up.

They flew over fields ...

seas ...

and mountains.

Finally they landed in the swallow's snug nest. Thumbelina was safe and happy at last.

Leapfrog has been specially designed to fit the requirements of the National Literacy Strategy. It offers real books for beginning readers by top authors and illustrators. There are 49 Leapfrog stories to choose from:

The Bossy Cockerel
ISBN 0 7496 3828 1

Bill's Baggy Trousers
ISBN 0 7496 3829 X

Mr Spotty's Potty
ISBN 0 7496 3831 1

Little Joe's Big Race
ISBN 0 7496 3832 X

The Little Star
ISBN 0 7496 3833 8

The Cheeky Monkey
ISBN 0 7496 3830 3

Selfish Sophie
ISBN 0 7496 4385 4

Recycled!
ISBN 0 7496 4388 9

Felix on the Move
ISBN 0 7496 4387 0

Pippa and Poppa
ISBN 0 7496 4386 2

Jack's Party
ISBN 0 7496 4389 7

The Best Snowman
ISBN 0 7496 4390 0

Eight Enormous Elephants
ISBN 0 7496 4634 9

Mary and the Fairy
ISBN 0 7496 4633 0

The Crying Princess
ISBN 0 7496 4632 2

Jasper and Jess
ISBN 0 7496 4081 2

The Lazy Scarecrow
ISBN 0 7496 4082 0

The Naughty Puppy
ISBN 0 7496 4383 8

Freddie's Fears
ISBN 0 7496 4382 X

FAIRY TALES
Cinderella
ISBN 0 7496 4228 9

The Three Little Pigs
ISBN 0 7496 4227 0

Jack and the Beanstalk
ISBN 0 7496 4229 7

The Three Billy Goats Gruff
ISBN 0 7496 4226 2

Goldilocks and the Three Bears
ISBN 0 7496 4225 4

Little Red Riding Hood
ISBN 0 7496 4224 6

Rapunzel
ISBN 0 7496 6159 3

Snow White
ISBN 0 7496 6161 5

The Emperor's New Clothes
ISBN 0 7496 6163 1

The Pied Piper of Hamelin
ISBN 0 7496 6164 X

Hansel and Gretel
ISBN 0 7496 6162 3

The Sleeping Beauty
ISBN 0 7496 6160 7

Rumpelstiltskin
ISBN 0 7496 6165 8

The Ugly Duckling
ISBN 0 7496 6166 6

Puss in Boots
ISBN 0 7496 6167 4

The Frog Prince
ISBN 0 7496 6168 2

The Princess and the Pea
ISBN 0 7496 6169 0

Dick Whittington
ISBN 0 7496 6170 4

The Elves and the Shoemaker
ISBN 0 7496 6575 0*
ISBN 0 7496 6581 5

The Little Match Girl
ISBN 0 7496 6576 9*
ISBN 0 7496 6582 3

The Little Mermaid
ISBN 0 7496 6577 7*
ISBN 0 7496 6583 1

The Little Red Hen
ISBN 0 7496 6578 5*
ISBN 0 7496 6585 8

The Nightingale
ISBN 0 7496 6579 3*
ISBN 0 7496 6586 6

Thumbelina
ISBN 0 7496 6580 7*
ISBN 0 7496 6587 4

RHYME TIME
Squeaky Clean
ISBN 0 7496 6588 2*
ISBN 0 7496 6805 9

Craig's Crocodile
ISBN 0 7496 6589 0*
ISBN 0 7496 6806 7

Felicity Floss: Tooth Fairy
ISBN 0 7496 6590 4*
ISBN 0 7496 6807 5

Captain Cool
ISBN 0 7496 6591 2*
ISBN 0 7496 6808 3

Monster Cake
ISBN 0 7496 6592 0*
ISBN 0 7496 6809 1

The Super Trolley Ride
ISBN 0 7496 6593 9*
ISBN 0 7496 6810 5

* hardback